# Snail's
# Good Night

by **ANN WHITFORD PAUL**

*illustrated by*
**ROSANNE LITZINGER**

Holiday House / New York

For Sarah with love
A. W. P.

For Giovanni
R. L.

Reading level: 1.9

Text copyright © 2007 by Ann Whitford Paul
Illustrations copyright © 2007 by Rosanne Litzinger
All Rights Reserved
Printed and Bound in Malaysia
The text typeface is Versailles.
The artwork for this book was created with watercolor, gouache,
and colored pencil on fine cold press watercolor paper.
www.holidayhouse.com
First Edition
1 3 5 7 9 10 8 6 4 2

Library of Congress Cataloging-in-Publication Data
Paul, Ann Whitford.
Snail's good night / by Ann Whitford Paul ;
illustrated by Rosanne Litzinger. — 1st ed.
p. cm.
Summary: When Snail realizes that his friends are going to bed,
he begins a very long, very slow slide to wish them all good night.
ISBN-13: 978-0-8234-1912-8 (hardcover)
ISBN-10: 0-8234-1912-6 (hardcover)
[1. Bedtime—Fiction. 2. Snails—Fiction. 3. Animals—Fiction.]
I. Litzinger, Rosanne, ill. II. Title.
PZ7.P278338Sna 2008
[E]—dc22
2007000614

Snail pokes his head
out of his shell.

"Bunny is not hopping,"
he says.

"Mouse is not running.
Sparrow is not flitting."

Snail waves his feelers.
The moon is moving up
in the dark blue sky.
The stars shine.
"My friends must
be going to bed,"
says Snail.
"I will go and
wish them good night."

Snail slides
slowly,
slowly,
slowly
over a leaf.

After a long time,
he reaches Bunny's den.

The sky is black.

The moon is high.

The stars shine.

Snail calls, "Good night, Bunny."

Bunny peeks out of her den.

She yawns.
"I was almost asleep,"
she says.
"Maybe Mouse is
almost asleep too," Snail says.
"I will hurry to Mouse."

The moon is low.
The stars still shine.
Snail calls, "Good night, Mouse."
Mouse rubs his eyes.

He says, "Snail!
You woke me up."
"I am sorry," says Snail.
"I hope Sparrow
is not asleep yet.
I must hurry to her."

Snail slides

slowly,

slowly,

slowly

across a rock.

After a long,

long,

long time,

Snail reaches Sparrow's tree.

The sky is bright blue.

The stars are gone.

The moon is gone too.

Snail calls,

"Good night, Sparrow."

Sparrow pecks at her feathers.
"Why do you say 'good night'?"
she asks.
"It is time to get up."

"I never went to bed," Snail says.
His feelers droop.

"Saying 'good night' is hard work.
Now *I* am tired."
Snail shrinks himself
small
and then smaller.

He shrinks himself
as small as he can.

Snail curls
into his shell
tight
and then tighter.

He curls into his shell
as tight as he can.
Bunny, Mouse, and Sparrow call,
"Sleep well, Snail!"
And Snail does sleep well . . .